The President's Glasses

For Mia with love

Gill Books
Hume Avenue
Park West
Dublin 12
www.gillbooks.ie

Gill Books is an imprint of M.H. Gill & Co.

© Peter Donnelly 2017, 2018
First published in hard cover 2017
First published in paperback 2018

978 07171 7540 6

Designed by www.grahamthew.com
Printed by L&C Printing Group, Poland

This book is typeset in Baskeville 32 pt.

The paper used in this book comes from the wood pulp of managed forests. For every tree felled, at least one tree is planted, thereby renewing natural resources.

THE PRESIDENT'S GLASSES

Peter Donnelly

Gill Books

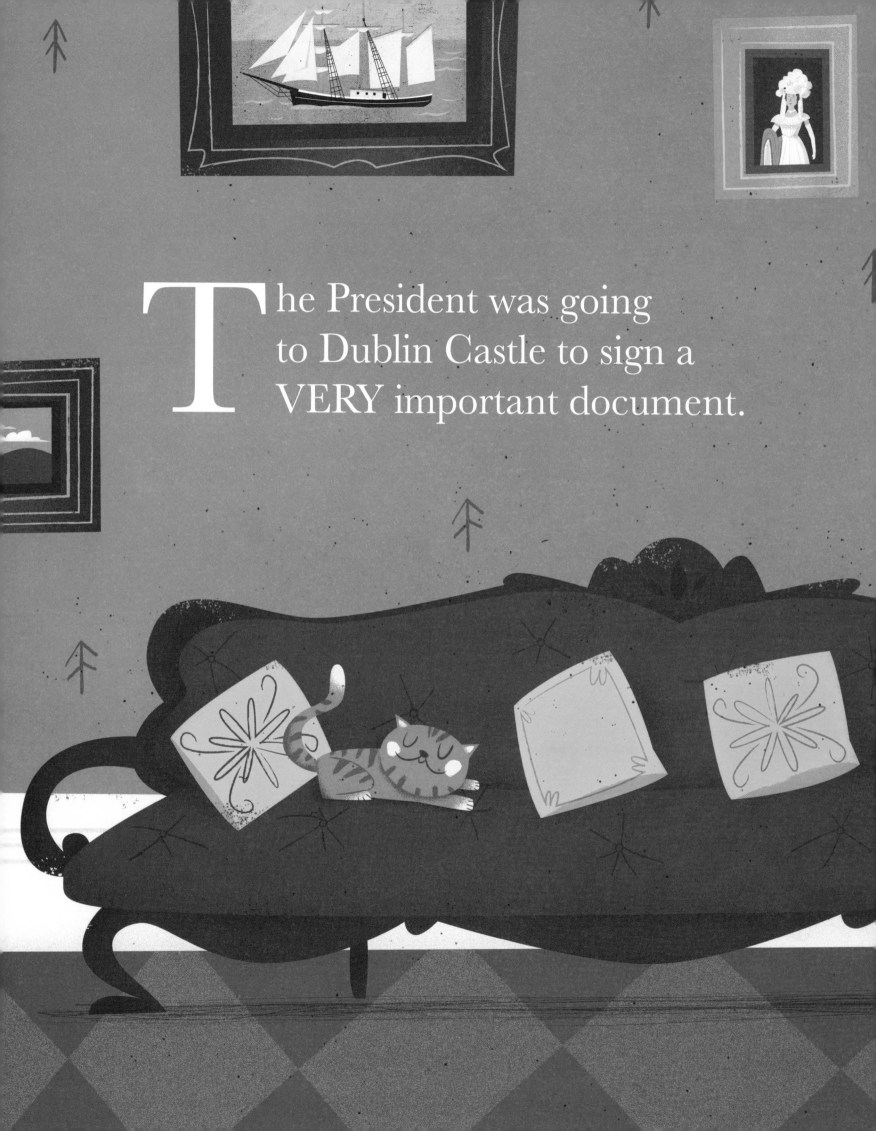

The President was going to Dublin Castle to sign a VERY important document.

But ...

... he left without his glasses.

'Oh dear!' said the President's wife. She handed the President's glasses to the President's pigeon and ordered him to fly to Dublin Castle IMMEDIATELY!

He flew high above the city to see if he could spot the President's car.

O'Connell Street was very
busy with people rushing to work.

The crowd bustled about and the traffic was ...

bumper

to bumper.

He flew across the River Liffey hoping to find the President's car, but instead he saw a boat race in the water.

A Viking ship was winning!

At Trinity College he
noticed a large crowd.

Perhaps the President was signing autographs?

Click!

Click! Click!

Click!

Next he **SWOOPED** past
Saint Stephen's Green …

TALANA   COLENSO

… but all he could see were his cousins enjoying a morning swim.

As he passed Christ Church Cathedral, the bells rang SO LOUDLY that he almost dropped the President's glasses with fright!

But he didn't ...   phew!

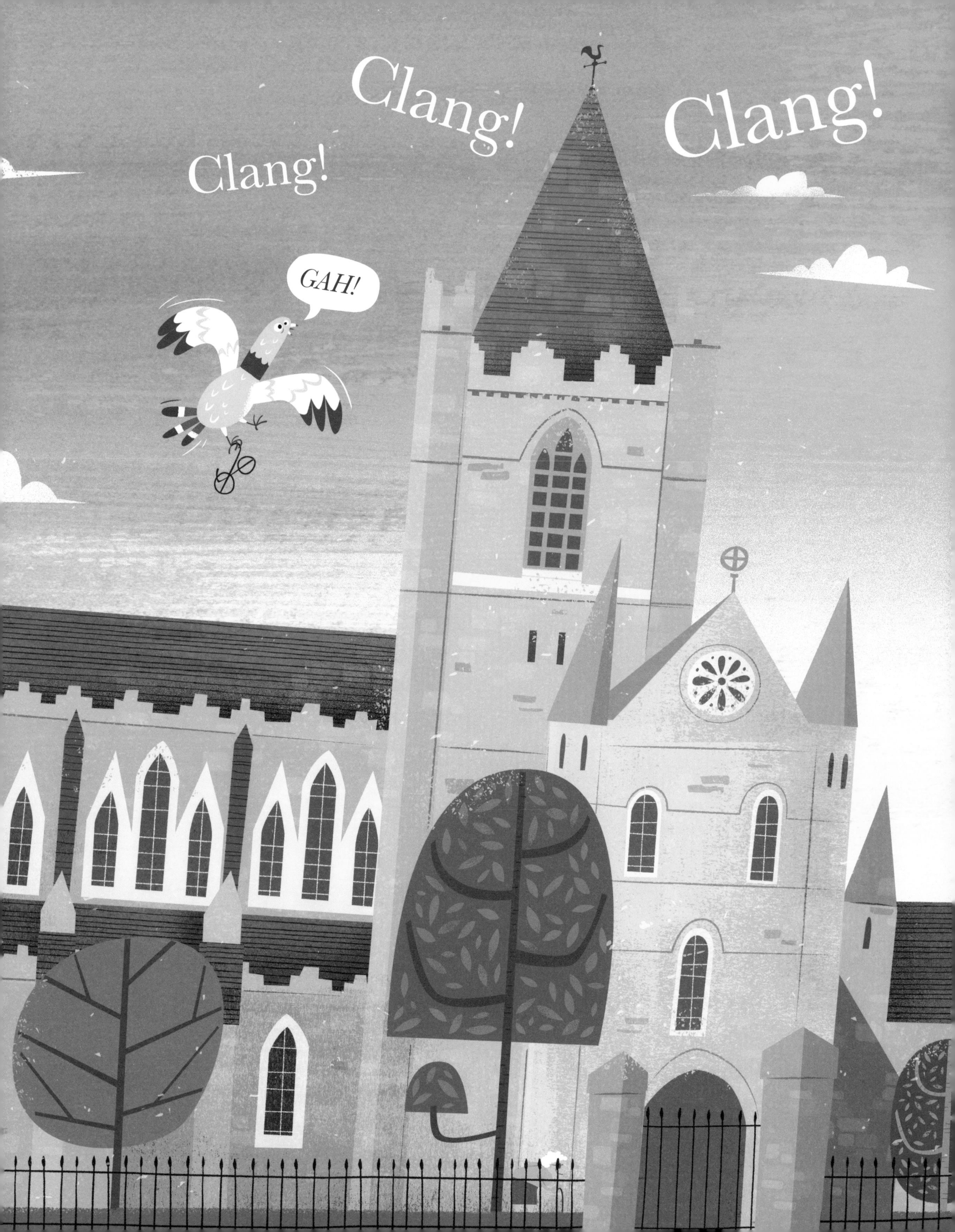
Clang!
Clang!
Clang!
GAH!

By now the President's pigeon was feeling a little bit tired …

... so he hitched a ride from a passing hot air balloon.

At last he made it to Dublin Castle where he spotted the President's car parked inside the gates.

Everybody CLAPPED and CHEERED as the President's pigeon landed safely on the President's desk with the President's glasses.

'Thank you, pigeon',
said the President as he
put on his glasses.

'Now where did I leave
my **blooming** pen?'

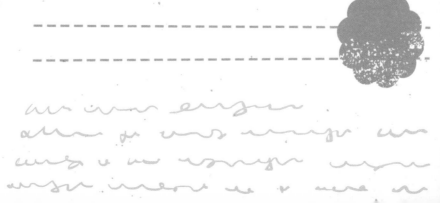